When Annie Dreams

MARY JOYCE LAWHORN

iUniverse, Inc.
Bloomington

When Annie Dreams

iUniverse books may be ordered through booksellers or by contacting:

iUniverse
1663 Liberty Drive
Bloomington, IN 47403
www.iuniverse.com
1-800-Authors (1-800-288-4677)

ISBN: 978-1-4697-8819-7 (sc)
ISBN: 978-1-4697-8820-3 (e)

Printed in the United States of America

iUniverse rev. date: 2/24/2012

Contributing Cover Photo; Caroline Wells Conkin

Summer of 1957

It hadn't rained a drop for over a month in southern Kentucky, and the heat was relentless, hovering just under 100 degrees. The night usually brought some relief from the sweltering days, though tonight no cool breeze blew through the open window where Annie lay awake, with only the moon light casting shadows across her nearly nude body. Even with no air stirring, she sought to catch a stray puff of wind by going over to the window, curling up in a worn out wicker chair. The ratty wicker was rough against her body as she struggled to get comfortable.

"Why?" she wondered. "Why do I stay in a God-forsaken place like this?" It seemed a lifetime ago that she married Thomas Flowers. He was why she was there, but she wasn't sure he was the reason she stayed.

"Annie, what are you doing sitting in the dark? "Come back to bed,"

Tom called out.

"It's too hot to sleep. I think I'll sit here for a while."

Tom grumbled that he had to get up early, then rolled over and went back to sleep. He was so exhausted from being in the fields all day, so much so that he didn't even miss her the rest of the night as she sat and waited for dawn to break.

Annie didn't know what was worse; sleeping in her soft bed sweltering all night or sitting by the window feeling the breeze blow against the beads of sweat on her body. She chose the latter; at least she would escape the heat for a few hours.

She felt the temperature rising even before the sun rose above the woods and wished she hadn't stayed up all night; at least she might have gotten some sleep. She thought about crawling back in bed and just sleep all day, but couldn't, because she had chores to do. One being their only source for milk, Betsy, their six year old Holstein would be waiting patiently in her stall to be relieved from her heavy udder.

The last of the sweet corn needed to be gathered, pulling the corn off the stalks, cleaning and all the other work it would take to get it ready wasn't what she dreaded; it was firing up the wood stove to cold-pack it. It would be unbearably hot and would take all night for the kitchen, as well as the whole house to cool down. She knew it would be another sleepless night for her.

The garden had all but dried up, except what little there was she had to salvage, yet she couldn't help but be relieved that there wouldn't be over a bushel of corn to prepare.

Tom had already gone out to the fields and Annie watched him holding on to old Jake's reins as the sway-back mule pulled the plow through the dry, hard earth, turning it for next year's crop. From the kitchen window she could see his shirt was already soaked with sweat and she was feeling guilty because she hadn't fixed him breakfast again. It wasn't so long ago she was up before the sun, baking biscuits, frying bacon and cooking up his eggs just the way he liked them. Now, she was too tired to even try, tired of the years of hard work that had taken its toil on their marriage, feeling every bit of fifty, rather than the thirty years she would be turning soon.

A knock on the screen door jolted her away from the sink full of corn she was cutting off the cob and the self-pitying thoughts she was having.

With the sun to his back, Annie was squinting to see who was there. She made out a tall figure of a man wearing a hat as she made her way down the hall.

When she opened the screen door she was taken aback by the stranger's dark good looks.

"Hi. My name is Edward Barns; I'm taking the county census this year… May I come in?" he asked, as he removed his hat to wipe beads of sweat from his forehead.

Blocking the glare of the morning sun with a dish towel she was still holding, she told him, "Well, I am really

busy right now; could you come back some other time?"
Suddenly aware of her calloused and chapped hands, she
dropped them to her side.

The man hadn't noticed her hands, but he knew she
must be preparing fresh corn, because bits of the yellow
mush had splashed on the pretty woman's cheeks. He
knew this from watching his grandmother cut corn off
the cob when he was a kid; he knew what a mess it would
make.

"Of course, there are several other houses I have to go
to today. Would tomorrow be better for you Mrs...?" he
paused, waiting for her to introduce herself.

"Annie... my name is Annie Flowers. Yes tomorrow
will be fine," she answered.

"Good deal, Mrs. Flowers. See you tomorrow around
10:00 am, if that's not too early for you?"

"Not at all, see you then." She answered back.

Annie caught a glimpse of her reflection in the mirror
as she passed by the vanity in the hall, and wished she had
at least combed her hair before pulling it back in her usual
ponytail, for she couldn't help but noticed how neat and
attractive Edward Barns was.

As she walked around the house with a bucket of
corn cobs to throw over the fence, her mind was still on
the unexpected visitor, and she almost bumped into her
husband.

"What was that city slicker doing way out here?" He
asked.

"That was Mr. Barns from the county census. But, I

don't think you would call him a city slicker; he lives in Monroe County."

"Where ever he is from, he didn't stay very long." Tom cut in, being rather short with his wife.

"Oh, he is coming back tomorrow. I told him I was too busy this morning."

Sullenly, her husband walked off mumbling. "That's a bunch of bull! Why does the county need to know a man's business for anyway?"

He drew a fresh bucket of water from the well and Annie watched her husband gulp down two full dippers before stopping, then pouring another dipper full over his head.

She wondered where the sweet man had gone, the man she had once loved so much. Guilt washed over her for even thinking about another man, after all, Tom was a good husband that worked hard and she knew the constant worry about making ends meet kept him in a bad mood; he didn't even seem like the man she married. She thought back to the days they worked in the fields together, when they were like kids and the work was fun. But that seemed like a hundred years ago to Annie.

Supper time came and went without much being said, which was the norm between Annie and Tom those days. Then, as usual, Tom went outside to the porch to light up his pipe. There he would sit or wander over to the barn until bedtime. Tonight, Annie would wash her hair and pamper her dried, cracked feet and hands, something she had neglected to do lately.

Annie awoke early so she could have her chores done before daybreak. By then her husband was already out in the fields somewhere, most likely on the north side.

She took her only good dress out of the closet to wear that day, then after applying a little makeup she looked in the mirror once again to smooth the unruly curls of her hair down.

It was only eight o'clock, so she still had time to tidy up the kitchen before Mr. Barns would be arriving. Before she knew it, it was almost ten o'clock, so she jerked her apron off and hurried to take another quick look in the mirror, "amazing, she thought, what a little makeup could do." But the sparkle in her eyes was more in anticipation for Edward Barn's visit than it was from the makeup. It had been a long time since she had company, and she was lonely for conversation, even if it was with a stranger who was coming there on business. Then she felt her face flush for being a silly woman with no life.

Mr. Barns arrived right on time, hoping he could get through with this last call so that he would have time to drive up to Lexington before it got too late. As he was about to knock, Annie opened the door.

"How do you do, Mrs. Flowers?"

"I'm doing very well Mr. Barns, thank you. Won't you come in?"

"Could I get you a cup of coffee or maybe some ice tea?" Annie asked when he was seated.

"No, I don't think so... on second thought, a cold glass of tea sounds pretty good if it's not too much trouble." In just a few minutes Annie returned with two tall glasses of sweet tea. She had already chipped small pieces from the huge block of ice that was delivered the day before, and had it ready in the icebox.

"Shall we get started?" There are several forms we will need to fill out, I don't want to keep you, so I'll try to make it as quick as possible."

"That's quite all right, Mr. Barns, please take all the time you need."

She thought he seemed to be in a hurry, and was disappointed that they couldn't just have some small talk outside of business. That made her feel even more foolish.

"Please call me Edward, "Mister" makes me feel old," he said smiling, showing the whitest teeth she had ever seen. He looked to be in his early forties, Annie thought.

"Only if you call me Annie," she smiled back.

Edward was thinking what an attractive woman Annie was, and envied her husband. He had been in a few relationships, but nothing ever came of them and he often thought he would remain a bachelor the rest of his life. He couldn't help but think the reason he hadn't met the right one, was because all the good ones were taken, for you didn't run across a beautiful woman like this very often. He felt his face getting red from his own thoughts, hoping she hadn't noticed.

Just as the census man was winding up his business, Tom came in for lunch, visibly upset because his wife hadn't even put his plate out. Then he walked on into the living room.

"You must be Mr. Flowers?" Edward said, standing up to shake his hand.

"That's right, I see you are getting ready to leave," Tom said, ignoring the visitor's extended hand.

"Annie, is there anything to eat in there? I've got to hurry and get back out, nighttime and taxes don't wait for nobody," he said, while glaring at Mr. Barns.

"I'm sorry if I kept you too long Annie. It was nice meeting you both, but I'll be on my way now." Mr. Barns said, apologizing for obviously upsetting the husband.

"It was nice meeting you too, have a safe trip," Annie said, as she walked him to the door.

"A safe trip? And Annie! That's real cozy; first name bases so soon. Was that part of his business telling you where he was going while he was here?" Tom asked sarcastically.

"He is a nice man, Tom. You didn't have to be so rude to him. No wonder no one ever visits us."

"And I could care less. I don't have time to socialize and neither do you."

Tom knew his wife wasn't happy these days, but he didn't know what she wanted from him. Seems he could do nothing to please her. He felt bad about snapping at Annie, for she didn't deserve that. No wonder she looks so sad all the time, he thought as he kicked the water bucked across the yard.

She had changed a lot since they married, a little less

than ten years ago. He could remember a time he was the only company she wanted, she didn't need to socialize then. Beside's that, she never dressed up for him anymore, noticing she had on a blue sundress he hadn't seen her wear in a long time.

Annie went into the bedroom and took off her good dress, throwing the old one over her head, which was threadbare and cooler anyways. She pulled her long red hair back with a rubber band as she was heading to the garden to gather the last of the red peppers. The sun was so hot it felt as if it sat on her head, even the straw hat didn't help. Sweat rolled off her face, taking with it the makeup she had applied so carefully earlier that morning, where now it was a streaking mess running down her chest. She never could stand the heat, which was worse now than she could remember it ever being in September. She wondered if Tom remembered it was her birthday.

*   *   *   *

The long hot summer days were coming to an end. Annie wasn't as busy with the garden gone, and all the chores that came with summer, so she would often take a walk down an old dirt road that ran through a wooded area. The deeper you went in there, the cooler it got, and it was nice letting her feet dangle in the cold spring water that ran out from a hidden cave. Had it not been for the running water, you would never know the cave was there.

Instead of thinking bad thoughts of her husband, she remembered when Tom took her to this very spot. He told her that when he was a boy that was where he would go when his parents were fighting, he would stay there for as long as he thought it would take for them to quiet down. He told Annie his father was a big man and was mean when he was drinking, but would also be as gentle as a lamb when sober. His mother had a temper too; Tom said. And she would fight back like a man. Once she hit her husband with an iron skillet that brought blood spurting out everywhere. It took fourteen stitches to sew him up. That's when his uncle Roy came and took him home with him for a week or so. After that Tom stayed with his uncle more than he did at home. It was hard for Annie to comprehend such goings-on. Being an only child and with no father around she was sheltered from most bad things of the world.

Annie didn't want to think of all the things going through her mind, so she concentrated on what a beautiful time of the year it was, with the leaves turning and falling down around her, sometimes getting caught in the curls of her hair, bringing back memories of when she once lived a carefree life growing up in New England. She wondered why we couldn't always see the world through the eyes of a child, even after we become adults. At least most children's eyes, she thought; thinking of Tom and what he must have experienced.

The sun would be going down soon. Annie knew she would have to hurry back before dark caught her in the deep of the woods where you couldn't see your hand in front of you after the sun went behind the distant hills. She knew how frightening it could be, for when she was ten years old; she had gone to Tennessee to spend the summer with her grandparents.

One day she decided to take a shortcut through the woods to pick wildflowers that she knew were in a field on the other side. She had gotten turned around and spent the whole night lost in the woods, similar to the woods that adjoined their property now. She remembered how relieved her grandfather was when he found her sound asleep in an old rotten tree that had fallen. He told everyone that story, how smart his granddaughter was to have taken refuge in such a place. She had used the hollowed out part for a bed. Besides a bunch of mosquito bites, she was fine.

As Annie exited the woods she was relieved to see the silhouette of their small farmhouse in the distance, once it came in to view she wasn't afraid anymore, so she took her time the rest the way home gathering up a few acorns along the way, and wishing for better days when she didn't even know what worry was. Once, she overheard her aunt Betty Jo and her mother Kate, having what seemed like a serious conversation. She heard one of them say, "If it's not one thing to worry about, it's two." Of course, that got the eight year old girls curiosity up; compelling Annie to ask her mother what the word "worry" meant.

"I hope you never have to know honey. Just enjoy being innocent and young." Not giving her daughter a clear answer left Annie with a dread of growing up, because she didn't want whatever it was that grown people got called "worry."

Well she did grow up; she knew now what her mother and aunt were talking about. It seemed that was all there was in life, one worry after another. She missed her mother now more than ever, because she realized that like herself, although in a different way, she must have had it rough. Being a single mother in those days wasn't accepted as well as it was now.

*   *   *   *

Annie and Tom weren't always unhappy, especially the first years of their marriage. Before they ever met, Tom had served in the army during the war, then, after the war ended he was shipped from France, back to the states. Instead of going back to his hometown, he went to work for an Army buddy whose family had a business in New England. That's where he met Annie. It wasn't long before they fell in love and got married. Right after the wedding, he quit his job of three years, and the young couple moved to Kentucky.

It had been a long time since Tom had been back home. In fact the day he buried his parents was the day he left and joined the army. He was only eighteen when the both of them were killed in a tragic accident. There was no reason to stay, so he boarded up the windows and doors, leaving everything the way it was.

After so many years being away the old cabin had gone down. It had been vandalized and not much was left. The windows were broken, letting in the rain to ruin the walls and floors. There was a lot of work to do if they planned on making it livable, so they spent their nights making love and their days fixing up the old house her husband's family had left him.

Life was good for a while, working side by side. They put in long hours painting the rough logs of the tiny cabin that had turned gray over time. In the afternoon, they would go skinny dipping down at the creek to cool off. Annie never complained about not having electricity or running water in the house. It was foreign to what she was used to, but they were young and in love, no longer children, yet not quiet adults either, for the thing Annie's mother called "worry" had not found them yet.

*   *   *   *

Tom was sitting on the porch as usual that time of day, with legs stretched out, puffing on his pipe. He had seen Annie coming down the lane, though he didn't even acknowledge her presence when she walked up. Instead he got up, stretched and walked out to the barn. He had been spending a lot of time out there in that old barn, Annie thought. She suspected he had some moonshine hid in the loft and was having himself a swig or two at night. It was just as well, she didn't want to know. She hated the smell of alcohol and there was no chance of them being close enough for her to smell it on his breath.

Tom could see their bedroom window from the barn and he watched his wife undress, as if she were a stranger, for he hadn't seen her nude in a long time, but he could still smell the sweetness of her soft red hair as it fell around her breasts, accentuating her flawless white skin that glistened from the light of the oil lamp. Unlike her hands, the rest of her body had not turned brown from the sun. Desire awakened for his wife and more times than he could count, he wished things were the same as they used to be. Just as quickly, anger and guilt replaced the want as he finished off the last bit of his moonshine, tossing the Mason jar hard against a rock he used for a doorstop; watching it shatter into a thousand pieces, just like his dreams had.

He didn't even work on the washstand he had been making for Annie as a surprise for her last birthday. He wanted so much to have it ready but working in the fields left him little time and energy to finish it, so he pretended he had forgotten she had turned thirty that day. He would finish it by Christmas for sure.

* * * *

The same old thing still haunted Tom's mind; the premature birth of their son. It had been seven years ago when Annie was in her sixth month. He knew his wife was working too hard, and he should have stopped her, made her rest. Then one day while they were clearing out a fence row his wife collapsed and the doctor told them she was lucky, a miracle really that she hadn't hemorrhaged to death, though she had lost the baby. The doctor strongly recommended they not try to have any more children. From that day forward, Tom went into himself, working every waking hour. The guilt was eating him up alive, keeping busy was the only way he knew how to deal with it, so he worked until he was so tired he couldn't think and occasionally, like tonight, he would drown it all in the liquor he had stashed away for times like this.

Annie had tried in the beginning to reassure her husband, telling him it wasn't his fault they had lost the baby, but deep inside, she did blame him. If he hadn't moved her way out in the country, things might have been different, but she, like her husband, felt the guilt as well, for not taking better care of herself. Added to that loss, was the struggle to keep the farm going from one month to the next, leaving little time to work on their marriage. How she longed to be that innocent, young girl again.

She pretended to be asleep when her husband finally came to bed. The long walk in the woods hadn't tired her as she had thought it would, and sleep didn't come easily. She could hear her husband stumble over something, cursing under his breath.

They were like strangers, both with their faces to the wall, not even touching. In just a few minutes she knew he was already asleep, because she could hear the even breathing of her husband before she finally drifted off; off to a place where the sky was as blue as the ocean and as the white clouds moved, it felt as if she were floating along with them on a cool green bed of moss, while a soft breeze tossed leaves around her and the man she was with.

He lay next to her winding a soft curl of her hair gently around his finger. She couldn't help but notice his eyes were as blue as the sky as he leaned over to kiss her. Waiting for his lips to take hers; anticipating what was to come made her tremble, but, like all the other times she would wake from her dream before she could feel the stranger's lips on hers. A stranger's lips, yet oh so familiar was his face.

Summer of 1959

It was almost the end of another summer, but unlike the last couple of years, it had been a beautiful and prosperous season. In fact, they had such an abundance of vegetables to sell, they could actually put some money aside.

Annie had somehow accepted her lot in life, and so had Tom. Even the handsome man that came to their house that day didn't cross her mind as often now, he was a distant memory that would occasionally visit her in a dream.

Things hadn't changed between Annie and Tom, except the resentment between them was gone now, but it was worse. Tom had rather felt the resentment or even hate from his wife, for it would have been better than feeling nothing at all.

How different things would have been, if we could have had more children, Tom would think sometimes. At other times, especially when he was drinking heavy, he thought about chucking it all in, leaving Kentucky and his life there for good. He wished he had never come back to his home town, and stayed in Maine where his wife had lived all her life. Maybe there he and Annie wouldn't have grown apart after they lost the baby. Strange as it was neither one of them couldn't imagine a life without the other.

*   *   *   *

Since they had such a good year and could afford it, Tom had asked his wife if she would like to go back to New England for a few weeks to visit her mother, he told her it might do her good to get away. Annie said she would think about it, but in the end she decided not to go. "Maybe next year." She told him.

Another reason she put it off was because Annie knew her mother had a full time job and traveled a lot and more than likely she wouldn't get to see her that much. There was no one else out there that Annie knew. What friends she used to have had moved away and they had lost touch years ago.

Tom had traded for a used pickup truck that winter. He thought it would at least get his wife to town and back each month to buy supplies for the farm or whatever else she needed.

Like today, Annie looked forward to the trips she made to Deer Ridge, population 3000. At least that was the count when someone placed the sign under the one that read, "Welcome to Deer Ridge, Ky." That sign had been there for ten years, maybe longer. Annie saw it the first day they moved there. She knew there had to be more people now than back then.

As she drove past the welcome sign once again, she wondered, "Why wasn't that changed last year when the census man was here?" She thought about Edward Barns, again. She wondered whatever became of him, but quickly chastised herself for thinking about a man who more than likely had a wife by now that he adored. She did notice that day he wasn't wearing a wedding ring though. For a while she fantasized about him coming back and taking her away, as the hero did in all the movies she had seen, rescuing the beautiful girl from whatever she needed to be rescued from. But unlike the girl in the movie, Annie did wear a wedding ring.

As always, her first stop in town was at the general store. There she could find anything from fabric to hardware. Walking across the long wooden porch, the first thing she saw in the store window was a beautiful water pitcher and basin set, displayed on a wooden table. She had not seen one of those since leaving New England; one similar to this one that her mother had brought over from France. The only time it was ever used was when company came. Then and only then, her mother would fill it with warm water and leave it in the guest bedroom. She missed her mother, for she hadn't seen her since she left home. The only contact was the letters they wrote each other.

When she entered the store, Annie walked over to the show window and ran her fingers over the white and blue snow-patterned enamel, admiring the piece that would be a luxury, rather than a need. She wondered if her mother still used her's only when company came.

"It is a beautiful piece isn't it, Mrs. Flowers? It just arrived today, all the way from France." Mr. Plews, the store owner said, startling her with his loud, boisterous voice as he walked up behind.

"Yes, it is Mr. Plews. My mother had one of those; it came from France as well." Then she said she thought they had not made any of those since the turn of the century.

"You are right about that Annie, but there is still some in stock and I can order a piece such as this for half of what it cost to make it."

"I can have it wrapped up and ready for you in a cat's wink. Only ten dollars and you can take that beauty home with you."

"Not today, Mr. Plews," she said, as he followed her around the store. I will take two yards of that yellow fabric and a spool of thread to match, if you have it," Annie told him, noticing there were several new rolls of cotton print that wasn't there last month.

After loading up the supplies for Annie, Mr. Plews

asked her again if she was sure she didn't want the enamelware.

"Its tempting, but I need other things more," she told him as she started up the truck. "Maybe next time." She smiled.

"See you next month, Annie." He called after her over the loud noise of the motor.

Mr. Plews was still smiling, thinking about Annie when his next customer came in. The man had waited across the street until Annie had left. He had watched as she admired something in the store window, then, when she drove off, he went over to the store.

"Good morning, Edward, what can I help you with today?" Mr.Plews never forgot a name. He remembered Edward from previous visits there. He also knew he took the county census a few years back and would often stop by for a sandwich and cold drink at lunch time.

"You may be able to help me out, Mr. Plews?" Edward said, pausing to scratch his head as if thinking what to say next.

"I saw a young lady in your store a while ago; I couldn't help but notice her admiring something in your window. Would you mind showing me what it was, please?"

"That's a strange thing for you to ask. Are you acquainted with the young lady?"

"Yes, as a matter of fact, I met Mrs. Flowers when I was taking the census here." He could see the storekeeper was confused and hurriedly explained, that it was a gift he was looking for a lady friend and wasn't good at picking women things out. That made sense to Mr. Plews, so he showed the wash set to Mr. Barns.

"Yes, Annie did like this piece, said it reminded her of the one her mother used to have," Mr. Plews said as he took it out of the window, holding it up for his customer to see.

When he started to put it back in its place, Edward told him to wrap it up so it would be suitable for shipping, but not before he could put a note with it. Mr. Plews was excited about the sale, but secretly he wished Annie could have afforded it.

*   *   *   *

A horn was blasting away outside. Annie wondered who in the world could it be. No one ever visited, the only vehicle she ever saw was the mail truck if she happened to be out front. Sure enough, it was the mailman, when he saw Annie he shouted, "A package for you, Annie."

She could see his toothy grin clear from the front door. "A package for me?" She thought out loud. "I never ordered anything, Mr. Green!" She told him to double check, for it had to be a mistake.

"Its no mistake, it shore is addressed to you. See here?" he said, pointing to the address label. "It says Mrs. Annie Flowers. That's you, aint it Annie?"

"Well, yes it is, but…." her voice trailed off. It was a heavy box, and she was curious to see what was inside. As soon as she got in the house, she put the package on the kitchen table, hesitating to open it. What if it was sent by mistake? What would she do then? She pulled a knife from the drawer and started cutting the box open, curiosity getting the best of her. Inside was something wrapped in brown paper.

"Oh My God!" she whispered. "It's the wash basin from Mr. Plews general store." As she ripped the paper off the other item, she saw it was the matching water pitcher. At the very bottom was a note. The only thing it said was, "Something pretty for a pretty lady."

"Mr. Plews!" It had to be him, she thought. He was the only person who was in the store; he saw how much I liked it. But why? That didn't seem like something Mr. Plews would do; he always seemed very frugal to Annie. Where else could it have come from? Then a thought came to mind. Next month would be their wedding anniversary; somehow Tom knew about the basin and pitcher and had it sent to her, but that was even more far- fetched than her originally thinking Mr. Plews had sent it. Tom never remembered their anniversary or her birthday for that matter.

Then she thought of the oak washstand she found sitting in the kitchen last Christmas morning. Now she knew for sure, it had to be from Tom. He got it for her to go with the washstand that he had made for her.

It made Annie sad, knowing it was as much her fault as it was her husbands for allowing their marriage to fall apart as it had. She wasn't an easy person to live with;

she harbored resentful feelings toward her husband, even though she tried not to verbally blame him for the loss of their child. She knew her actions spoke louder than any words could have.

It didn't matter now anyway. There had been too many years of bitterness eating away at what they once had. She couldn't remember the last time they made love or showed each other any affection.

Annie carefully placed the beautiful basin and pitcher on the washstand, but, it looked so out of place to her, as much out of place as she had felt for so long in her marriage.

Annie didn't thank her husband for the gift, for it was late when he finally came in from the fields, going straight to bed after washing up, not even bothering to eat the plate of food she had kept warm for him.

*   *   *   *

Another month came around, and it was time for Annie to make her regular trip to town. After making out a list, Annie went out to where her husband and Roy was working on a broken fence to see if she had all the things he needed written down.

She was glad the man was at the very end, working his way up. Roy was a sharecropper, a big built man who looked to be in his early sixties. Annie had never talked to him; actually she didn't even know his last name.

Annie always made extra for him when he was there working through dinner, but he never came in to eat, just sat out in his old pickup truck. Tom told his wife he guessed he brought his dinner with him. She thought it was just as well, because she didn't like the way he always stared at her. Tom never seemed to notice. Even now, Annie could see him looking at her from under his wide brimmed hat. That piercing look made her skin crawl.

Tom stopped what he was doing, just looking at his wife for a long moment. He had aged so much, she thought. The years spent working in the fields under the hot sun had worn creases through his brow like trenches, where sweat ran through them, rolling off onto his face. Then he asked her, "Annie, when are we going to quit living this charade as husband and wife? Don't you think its time we stop tormenting each other and go our separate ways?"

She wondered if her husband and the sharecropper had been in the moonshine again. She had seen them taking a nip before when they didn't know she was looking.

Even if her husband was drinking, Annie was shocked to actually hear her him say what she knew already, but even more so to hear the defeat in his voice. She didn't know how to answer him, so instead she turned and walked away.

As she drove out of the drive, tears rolled down her face; she didn't know why. Was it because she would miss this place, a place that she had called God-forsaken? Was it Tom? Had she gotten so used to him that he had become a part of her?

Annie cried all the way to town. It was as if a dam had burst and all the years of frustration were gushing out.

Before she realized it, she had pulled up in front of the store, just as she did every first Monday of the month; she knew she would go to the mill for feed when she was through shopping; she would stop and get a chicken sandwich and coke at the only hamburger place in town, and just like every first Monday of the month, she would drive back home.

There was no way to hide her swollen eyes, so she kept her head down as much as possible, which that in itself drew attention to her from Mr. Plews.

"Annie, what on earth is the matter with you? You are as pale as a ghost…are you not feeling well? Here, sit down." he said, leading her to the nearest chair.

"I'm fine Mr. Plews, really I am. I must look a sight, worse than I really feel." Her attempt to reassure Mr. Plews wasn't working, so she didn't say anything more. Instead, she put her head down as the tears started rolling uncontrollably again. Mr. Plews didn't try to stop her, but let her cry it all out. He knew from his own experience how women were. He had been married to the same woman for fifty some years before she was taken from him. She was a good soul and worried about everything and everybody and her husband knew the best thing to do when his wife was sad, was just let her cry until she felt better, so he left Annie alone while he went about his business.

Finally, Annie pulled herself together and by this time Mr. Plews had gathered everything up that she had on her list. She was thankful that no other customers had come in. Then, after thanking him for everything as she was leaving, out of the corner of her eyes she could have sworn she saw someone she knew drive by.

"Was that him?" she thought for a fleeting second. It looked a lot like the handsome census man, but she thought it was her eyes playing tricks on her because she had been so upset. Mr. Plews was still standing on the porch, so Annie turned around and asked him if he saw the man who just drove past the store.

"Yes, of course. That was Edward Barns. He lives in Monroe County, the next County over. He comes by pretty regularly. Just last month, as a matter of fact, he came in the store right after you left and asked about the pitcher and bowl you were looking at. Said he wanted to buy someone a present, but wasn't very good at picking out something for a woman. I made a sale, thanks to you, Annie!"

"You sold them to Mr. Barns! The same pieces I was looking at?" Annie thought she had heard wrong.

"I'm so sorry. I felt bad about that, knowing you liked them, but I didn't know you were planning on buying them, if I had known I would have put the things in lay-away for you." He was sure that Mrs. Flowers was going to start crying again.

"No, that's not it. I thought my husband… never mind," she said and before making another scene, got in her truck and left poor Mr. Plews with a puzzled look on his face.

"Women," he said to himself. "God love- em."

If Mr. Plews was puzzled, it wasn't anything compared to what was going through Annie's head. She tried to remember if Tom had said anything about the package she received or commented on anything being different about the water stand. She did remember telling her husband how much she wanted the set, but felt she couldn't afford it. He shrugged his shoulders and said, something to the effect that, if she was happy with it, that was all that mattered. Nothing else was said, and she assumed he had it sent to her.

But why? She thought; why would Edward Barns buy her a gift? A man she had only met twice even though she had dreamed about him for months after that. He didn't know. How could he? By now she was confused as well as mad, because she had been wrong about her husband, so naive in thinking he had bought her a gift; confused as to why Edward Barns had.

As she passed the city limit sign "You are now leaving Deer Ridge," she could see a car pulled over on the side of the road with the emergency lights blinking. It looked a lot like the car she saw go by the general store. When she got up even with the parked car, sure enough it was Edward waving her down. Annie's heart starting pumping so hard she could almost hear it. She had a few things she wanted to say to him, so she pulled up in front of his car and waited to see if he was going to get out.

"Annie, I want to talk to you!" He called out. "Why don't you pull your truck in that little dirt road, just around the curve, and I will pick you up?"

"Well, I want to talk to you, too, Mr. Barns!" she answered back.

Throwing all caution to the wind, Annie pulled in the dirt road and got out of her truck and into the passenger's side of Edward's car.

"Mr. Barns, I know you sent me a package, what I want to know is, why?" She was mad and confused, but mostly her heart was in her throat from being so close to him.

"Please let me explain Annie. It was an impulse thing, and then I had second thoughts about it. In the end I decided what harm would it be? I am sorry if it upset you."

"Why didn't you just come over the day I was in town and speak? You know that is a little creepy to say the least! Spying on me like that!"

"I wasn't spying; you make me sound like a stalker."

"What else would you call it? How did you know I would be in town that day? Have you been stalking me?" Annie was beginning to feel a little uncomfortable now, sitting in a car with a man whom she barely knew.

"Hear me out Annie." He then told her how he couldn't get her off his mind. "I knew you were a married woman, but I have thought about you every day since we met." He paused a second, afraid Annie would get out of the car before he finished what he had to say. "You think

I am some kind of nut running around, don't you? I know you have every right to think that, but I just had to see you, then one day I happened to be in town and saw you going into the general store."

"You mean you saw me there more than once and didn't make yourself known?" Annie asked.

"I couldn't get the nerve to come over; I thought it might embarrass you for one thing."

"You got your nerve up this time. Why now?" She suspected he had seen her crying. If he only knew about the dreams she had of him.

Why don't we go for a walk? There is a field of clover in the middle of the woods, just over that ridge. Do you have to get back home right away?" he asked her, almost with a pleading look.

"Not for a while. I do need to get some air; sure, why not?" She wasn't nervous anymore for it seemed she had known him for years. As a matter of fact, she hadn't felt carefree like that in a long time as they walked in the field of soft clover barefooted. She didn't care about the package now, and was secretly happy he had sent it to her. Like a love story, he was her hero in shining armor… coming to rescue her.

Not long into their walk, without any hesitation, Edward asked Annie why she was so sad. "Not only now, I saw it in your face the first day I laid eyes on you."

Annie didn't answer him; it wasn't the right time. Anyway, she suspected he knew she wasn't happy in her marriage, and besides that, she felt guilty even talking to Edward about her husband.

"I don't know why I am here with you, Edward; it's about as hard for me to know that as it is for you to know why you sent me a gift."

"Maybe all this was meant to be. Do you believe in predestination, Annie?"

"I've never thought about it before, do you believe that's what this is?" Annie asked, as he took her hand, pulling her down beside him.

"I think it may be. I have looked for someone like you all my life; I just never dreamed that someone could be as beautiful."

He was looking down at her now, holding a lock of her long red hair between his fingers, just like in her dream. She couldn't help but notice that his eyes were the color of the sky above them. At that moment she knew without a doubt what would come next, but this time she wasn't dreaming, and if she was, she hoped it never ended. They lay wrapped in each others arms for a long time afterwards, without speaking at all. They didn't have to; their hearts were speaking for them. Then Annie knew she had to go, the sun was going down and it was an hour drive back home.

"When will I see you again? Will I see you again?" he rephrased the question, not taking anything for granted.

"Of course, you will see me again. I don't know when I can get away, but it shouldn't be a problem." She never told him what her husband had said that day about them separating, and that was the reason she was so upset. She didn't understand her own feelings, much less try to explain them to Edward. By all accounts, she and Tom separated years ago; the only difference was neither one left. She didn't want anything to ruin the moment, so she never told Edward.

Edward was somewhat surprised that Annie didn't think it would be a problem for her to get away, remembering how possessive her husband seemed that day a few summers ago.

"Can you come here next week, to this same place?" he asked, praying she would say yes. Even a week was too long for him to wait for them to be together again.

"Do you know the owners of this property? I would hate to get run off by some angry farmer." Annie laughed.

"I don't think that will happen Annie. This is part of my uncle's farm, so we will be completely safe here."

As they walked back to where they had parked, Edward told Annie a little bit about his uncle. He was a sixty five year old confirmed bachelor. He had been jilted years ago when he was only nineteen by a girl named Beth whom he met while working in Joe's Diner. They were to be married the same day she left Deer Ridge.

The story goes; she caught a bus to California and never looked back. She was raised by a drunken father who never heard from her again, as far as anyone knew, and was more than likely happy to be rid of her. But, according to Edward, his uncle never got over her, so when his parents died he stayed on at their farm, trying to scratch out a meager living there. He went on to tell her how Roy had been like a father to him all his life. In fact, he bought him the first car he had ever owned. Annie could see how much his uncle meant to him.

*   *   *   *

Annie was a virgin when she met Tom. She had been with no other man up until now. Somehow, she didn't feel guilty, as if she and Edward had done anything wrong, instead, she felt young and alive again. Had someone been looking in, they would immediately think she was a Jezebel, sleeping with a man she had met only briefly. A married woman having a fling on the side! Was what they would say.

The house was dark when she pulled up the drive. The double doors to the barn were closed, and the long wooden plank was secured through the latch on each door, so she figured Tom wasn't in the barn, unless he went in the back way. He probably had gone to bed early, she thought, or maybe he had already left her.

The thought of her not having to face her husband brought relief to Annie. She just knew if he saw her he would know she had been with another man. Her relief was short lived, for Toms clothing were still hanging in their closet, but he wasn't in the house anywhere. His hunting rifle hadn't been moved, either. He would not have left without his personal things, at least not for long.

Annie assumed he had pulled in the back of the barn and more than likely drinking himself into a stupor.

The next morning, Annie was awakened by the bright sun shining on her face. She knew by the sun being that high it was late and she had to hurry to get old Betsy milked.

There was still no sign of Tom. She would check to see if his car was in the barn or not. When she opened the doors the car was not there, but Betsy was, waiting patiently in her stall to be milked. There was a back opening to the barn that led to a fenced in field so the cattle could come and go when they wanted to get out of the cold winters, or just to escape the heat or rainstorms of summer. Annie thought that must have been the way Tom drove out.

As she looked around for any sign of her husband, she saw his old work coat thrown across a bale of hay and an empty jar that had toppled over a few feet away. She was right in thinking he was in the barn drinking moonshine until he passed out and slept in the barn all night. Then he had left before she got out of bed.

Before leaving the barn Annie opened the shed door to put some hay out for Betsy, when she did she came face to face with some sort of dead animal hanging from the rafters; falling backward to get away, she dropped the bucket of milk; screaming! She ran as fast as she could to the house, hoping now Tom was somewhere around. She was still shaking from fright and being soaked with the milk. She locked every door and made sure all the windows were latched down before changing into something dry. By this time she was getting her senses back and was trying to figure how that animal got there. After a while she went to the closet and got her husband's gun, Just in case someone was out there trying to scare her. She headed to the barn.

"If you are in there you had better show your face or I will shoot that shed to hell!" Annie screamed as loud as she could.

When she was pretty sure no one was in the barn she slipped in and opened the shed door. There was a huge opossum hanging by the neck from a rope, and its throat had been cut. It was a terrible sight. Annie didn't know what to think of it and why someone would do that to a poor animal much less using it to scare her. Well, whoever did, succeeded, but she wasn't scared now; she was mad and if someone she didn't know showed up they would come face to face with the rifle she kept by her. "I will give them some of their own medicine." Annie thought to herself.

Before going back to the house she walked out to the back of the barn where nothing seemed to be out of place. There were tire tracks leading out of the barn which she suspected was her husband's when he left. Then, she glanced over to the side and saw where grass was mashed down; someone had pulled in and made a circle in the field going back out. Whoever it was knew the way in from the back road to the barn.

She wondered who would be prowling around like that,

especially if they knew Tom would be around somewhere. Maybe her husband had already gone, Annie thought. She knew the animal had not been there long because the blood that had dripped from it had not coagulated. It made her shake to think she was asleep and a stranger was right outside doing such an evil thing. What was even more frightening for her to think it could have been someone they knew.

It was going on twelve noon and Annie was still jumpy from that morning, and several times she thought she heard something outside .Tom hadn't showed up either; maybe he took his lunch with him, she thought. Sometimes he did that to save time, especially if he was working on the back side of the farm.

She knew he had been putting up a new fence around one of the pastures back there, and it would be late before he came back if that was where he went.

"He is a grown man and can take care of himself," Annie kept telling herself the rest of the day. "Anyway," she thought, "he isn't concerned about me being all alone, way out here. Then why should he be, she thought, as guilt tugged at her conscience for what she had done. In God's eyes she was an adulteress, regardless what condition her marriage was in or how she and Edward felt about each other.

To keep her mind off things she decided to sew. She propped the old rifle against the wall and raised the cherry wood top back that she used for a table when she wasn't sewing, and pulled out her treadle sewing machine. She would cut out the new piece of fabric to make a dress to wear when she saw Edward again, though she had just chastised herself for doing just that.

Edward wished Annie had a phone, but only a few people in the south had one. Some phone lines had been run through a few counties but hadn't reached as far as Deer Ridge, much less where Annie lived. He wanted to hear her voice, but he would have to wait. That he could do; he could wait forever for her. He wondered what Annie would tell her husband, the reason for going back to town so soon. He could only imagine what Tom Flowers would do if his wife crossed him. He seemed like an angry man with a mean temper, and capable of hurting her.

The very thought of someone hurting Annie made him sick, especially if it was because of him. He wished he hadn't made plans to meet her now, but the need to be with her overpowered his reasoning at the time and could have put her in danger. Edward knew he was letting his imagination run wild; he had to get a grip. He knew where Annie lived. He would try and check on her, maybe drive by. Then he thought better of that. "What would she think if she saw me?" Remembering what she said about him following her. All night he had dreams about Annie, They would be in a field making love, but someone was watching them. He couldn't make out who it was, but needless to say it was a restless night.

*   *   *   *

Meanwhile, almost two days had passed with no sign of Tom. Annie was getting worried now. "What if he had an accident and was hurt someplace, or worse?" She got in her truck and drove all over the fields where she thought he might have parked the car on the side of the road and walked across to wherever he was working. There was only one place with signs he had been there.

A coffee cup had been placed on top of one of the fencepost where he had been. As she held the tin cup in her hand, she saw the coffee had dried around the inside bottom, turning dark black. She knew it had been there over a day or two.

She tossed the cup in the back of the pickup and took off again. He was nowhere to be found so all she knew to do was to drive into town and talk to the sheriff. Then she thought how mad he would be if he had left to get away for awhile and the police came looking for him. After all, he did say they should separate. She could just imagine all the gossip there would be when this got out.

Annie went back to the house. She had to decide what to do. It would be getting dark in three or four hours, so she had to make her mind up in a hurry. Just as she ran out the door, a brown early model car pulled up and her husband stumbled out; waved at the driver and walked on to the house as if he hadn't even been gone. She couldn't remember ever seeing the car around there before, and the driver was too far away to make out who had brought her husband home.

Annie was furious. "Thomas Flowers! Where have

you been?" He looked awful, and where was his car? She thought.

"What the hell do you care where I've been?" He shoved on past her, reeking of alcohol. "I don't ask where you go, do I?" he said, slurring his words. She had never seen him in that kind of shape.

He looked straight through her, with eyes as dark as coal. It was then she saw a huge gash just above his eyebrow. It had bled quiet a bit because dry blood covered the front of his shirt. She followed him in the house almost afraid to say anything else to him. Annie couldn't help but feel sorry for the man she had lived with for so long, so her instincts were to get a wet washcloth to clean his cut, but when she tried, he started cursing again, turning into a madman. She remembered what he had told her about his dad and how mean he got when he was drinking.

"Get out of my way, you damn bitch!" He took a swing at Annie and lost his balance. When he hit the floor, he didn't get up. All the years she had known Tom, he had never been violent toward her, even when he was drinking. Annie wondered if he had found out about her being with Edward.

She kept her distance while trying to see if he was breathing. She could see he was, but apparently had passed out. She went to the closet, grabbed a quilt to throw over him. Then she went to her room and locked the door, trying to figure out what to do. For the first time she was scared of her husband. She thought about going to find Edward, but it would be dark before she drove into town. Also, she wasn't familiar with the roads in Monroe County. She would get lost for sure. She decided to stay there until morning. Then she would slip out and leave.

All night, she kept Tom's rifle next to her bed, although she had never shot a gun before, much less turn one on her own husband. She would shoot in the air to scare him if he came in on her, she decided.

Around three in the morning, she had just dosed off, when something hit the door hard, breaking it down. It was too dark to see who or what it was. She grabbed the gun, pointing it toward the ceiling and starting pulling on the trigger, but it wouldn't fire. Before she knew what happened, someone very strong grabbed the gun, hitting her with it across the back. Sharp pains ripped through her body before she passed out.

The next thing she knew she had come to, but she wasn't in her room. She didn't know how she got there, but she could see several nurses standing around. She couldn't move but could see tubes running from her arm and realized she was in a hospital. Annie tried to get someone's attention, but no words would come out." God, please don't let me be paralyzed," she prayed.

*   *   *   *

She wondered where Tom was. Then she remembered being attacked. He had to be the one who did this to her. She didn't know if she was screaming or thought she was, but two nurses came running and one of them stuck her with a needle, while the other one was trying to calm her, telling her that she was going to be all right. No one was going to hurt her there.

Annie didn't remember much of anything that happened to her just prior to the attack. Sometimes, she thought she was in the woods, lost as she was when she was a kid. Then her dreams of the dark woods would fast-forward to another nightmare where someone was over her, and she couldn't get him off. He was smothering her with his sweaty body. There was no pain, just the heaviness on her small frame, and with darkness all around.

There was always someone there to comfort her. She could feel gentle hands on her forehead as her mother's soft voice tried to calm her, though, she felt the safest when she knew Edward was there with his strong hands massaging her arms and legs; she couldn't feel them, but she could see. Neither could she speak, but her heart spoke to him. Edward seemed to know everything Annie was thinking and would reassure her until her fears went away. Only then, she would go back to sleep. He never left her side all the time she was in and out of the coma, except to shower and change. He vowed he would never leave her.

*   *   *   *

Thomas Flowers was found in a field two days after he allegedly attacked his wife. He was leaning against the same post where Annie had found the tin cup, with a single bullet to his head. It was ruled a suicide. Some folks around town didn't believe that, even though his rifle was still in his hand.

Later that same week, his car was found abandoned twenty miles from his house. There were no signs of foul play, and the police believed he just ran out of gas and hitched a ride home. The pathologist's report showed he had a concussion, which would explain his unusual behavior toward his wife the day he came home with his clothes bloody and smelling of alcohol. He had apparently been hit with some sort of blunt object, causing the gash on his head, knocking him out for hours. With no more to go on, the police suspected he may have gotten in a fight with someone, but since the injury to his head was not the actual cause of death, they left it as a self- inflicted gunshot wound that killed him. The detective speculated that he most likely was so distraught after he realized what he had done to his wife, that he took his own life.

After Annie was well enough, she was told about her husband's death, which she took very hard. She blamed herself for a lot of things. She knew Tom was a good man, before that terrible day he turned on her. The both of them were victims of circumstances; at least that's what the therapist told her. She told Annie she had seen the same thing happen to other couples during her career, marriages falling apart after the death of a child or some other tragedy. That didn't ease the guilt that Annie felt;

she blamed herself for not trying harder to save their marriage.

Annie's mother, Kate, had flown to Kentucky as soon as she got word her daughter was found brutally raped and almost beaten to death in her own bed. Since Kate was her next of kin, she was told everything that had happened to her daughter. Annie had been hit across the back, leaving her paralyzed. They didn't know if it would be permanent.

Like Edward, Kate wouldn't leave her side until she came out of the coma. It was during that time she learned about the relationship that had been developing between Annie and Edward. Reading between the lines, over the years she had suspected her daughter hadn't been happy in her marriage.

Four weeks into Annie's hospital stay, the doctors discovered she was pregnant. When they talked to Kate, they told her that her daughter may lose the baby because of having a premature birth before, not to mention the trauma she had endured. At that time there was little hope she would walk again, much less carry a baby full term.

All the doctors had said that there was less than fifty percent chance that she would ever walk again. Annie beat the odds and walked out of the hospital on her own in three months. Edward took her home with him and they married soon after because of the baby. There was talk at first as there always is in such a small town, because Tom was well respected the folks thought she should have waited longer.

Mr. Plews stood up with them as they said their wedding vows at the local courthouse in Deer Creek.

*　　*　　*　　*

Annie had no idea that Edward lived in such a beautiful home. He had never told her he was a wealthy man, and she never had a clue because, after all, he was a working man when they met. He told her later on that he had made his fortune in real estate and had made good choices in the stock market. Then one day he became tired of the city and the rat race. So with his real estate connections, plus Kentucky being the place he was born and raised. That was where he decided to settled. He had lived in Kentucky about seven years when he first met Annie.

Annie couldn't help remembering that Tom had called the census man a city slicker that day that seemed so long ago. Guess he was right after all. She thought.

Annie didn't understand why his uncle Roy had to work so hard, and why hadn't her husband helped him since they had always been so close. Edward explained.

"Uncle Roy is a proud man, even if he needed help he wouldn't ask for it, but the fact is, he has money and still chooses to work. He was never used to the finer things growing up and he never wanted them, even when he could afford it."

Then he told Annie that he supposed he was a lot like

his uncle as far as keeping busy. That's why he took the census job.

"But unlike my uncle, I do enjoy the things I have worked for." And he told his wife what was his, is theirs now.

*   *   *   *

No one told Annie she had been raped that night. If Annie didn't remember, no one was to tell her. Kate made that decision when she found out her daughter was pregnant. She felt Annie had been through enough without the added burden of knowing she could have conceived under such horrible circumstances. She kept the rape from everyone, with the exception of her doctor, no one knew. Kate found some comfort when the little boy was born, for then she was sure the baby belonged to Edward Barns, because he had eyes as blue as the sky and was the spitting image of his father.

Annie dared to dream she would have her own little baby because of what her doctor had told her after her miscarriage. Her mother called him "A miracle baby" Kate stayed with her daughter and Edward for a few weeks to help out. But it seemed being a mother came natural to Annie. And Kate felt Eddie Jr. was in good hands when she went back home.

That was only one of many trips that the new grandmother made to Kentucky. She was there on every birthday and all holidays. Edward would kid her and say, "Nanny, why don't you just move down here; it would be a lot cheaper for you." Of course the whole family wished she would. But Kate couldn't see herself a permanent resident in such a small town. But she would tell them. "I may surprise you one day; you never know!"

Annie never suspected there was a possibility their only son could belong to anyone but Edward, how could he not be? She had not had sexual relations with anyone but him for months before she got pregnant, not even her husband.

She never recalled all that happened to her that night, though she still had nightmares of the attack, just like the dreams she had before, except, for the last couple of years they were different. It was Tom who was trying to save her from someone else in her room. She could hear him call out her name. "Annie! Oh God, Annie, what has he done to you?" That's when the heavy weight was lifted off her and she could breathe again.

She would wake up calling Tom's name, trying to tell Edward about the nightmares. He would hold her as he always did, a hero in shinning armor, always there to rescue the damsel in distress, even from her dreams and the horrors her late husband left behind.

*   *   *   *

The day Eddie Jr. turned sixteen; his dad had a surprise for him. It was over at his Uncle Roy's house. It wasn't unusual for them to visit his uncle together because Roy always made a big deal out of it if Edward came over without little Eddie. This day was no different, except this was the day they were going to give Eddie his dad's old car. Uncle Roy had kept his nephew's first car in the barn all those years under a tarp. Edward knew that his Uncle Roy would take it out for a spin occasionally, but hadn't seen it for a while and was surprised at how good a shape it was still in. Eddie wanted to paint it candy apple red as soon as he saw it. His dad didn't blame him because he never liked the dull brown color either, but before they did do a new paint job, Edward wanted his Annie to see what the first car he ever owned looked like. Roy looked a little pale when he told him that maybe he should wait until they got it fixed up and painted, but Edward said that was the whole idea, for her to see it the way it originally looked.

A few weeks after she and Edward married, he took his wife out to meet the uncle he had talked about so much. She had no idea before that day that he was the same creepy Roy who had helped her late husband on the farm. She tried to make conversation by saying she remembered him being out there a few times, but he mumbled something she didn't understand. After that, she wasn't around him much. He was her husband's uncle and surely he had to be harmless, although weird; she reasoned to herself and never told Edward he made her feel uncomfortable, knowing, how close he was to his uncle it would break his heart if he knew how she really felt about him. She didn't like the way Roy still looked at her, but what most concerned her was how obsessed he seemed with Eddie.

Annie was hanging her wash on the clothes line when she looked up to see a car coming down the gravel road leaving a trail of dust that she just knew would settle on her fresh white sheets, but when the car stopped, luckily the wind was blowing in the opposite direction, to her relief.

She was surprised to see Edward get out the driver's side and her son jumping out trying to be the first to show his new car to his mother.

Annie was experiencing déjà vu. Hardly hearing what either one was saying to her. All she could do was remember a car exactly like this one that someone had driven her husband home in that awful day years ago.

"You look as if you have seen a ghost Annie." Edward said, seeing the strange expression on her face.

"Mom, this is dad's old car, the first one he ever owned! Uncle Roy has had it in his barn all this time, now they have given it to me, and Mom, we are going to paint it candy apple red! It's going to be a beauty. Right dad?"

"It sure is son. Why don't you run in the house while I talk to your mom."

"I get to keep it, don't I mama?" Eddie asked, not expecting this kind of reaction from his mother.

"What in the world is wrong with you Annie?" Edward asked, hoping she wasn't upset that their son would be driving soon.

After Annie found her bearings, she sat down on the steps, thinking she would pass out any time. Then she told her husband that the car was the same car that someone drove her husband home in the night she was attacked.

"There are other cars the same color around here. I wouldn't think Uncle Roy took him home, he would have said something to the police after all that happened, especially after Thomas was found dead."

It seemed to Annie; Edward was second guessing what she had just said.

"Edward, I will never forget that car, I am sure it is the same one!" Annie felt sick, as if she were going to throw up.

"Honey, do you really think my uncle had something to do with Thomas's death? Surely you can't believe that. As far as I know they didn't even know each other."

"Yes Edward, they did, he used to work out on the farm. I recognized him the day you introduced us, I tried to tell him that I had met him before but he shrugged me off. So I never brought it up again."

Edward knew his wife had been through a lot, he also knew that sometimes she didn't remember things exactly as they happened shortly before and after her attack. She was wrong about his uncle, there was no way he would harm a fly; A little exocentric but harmless.

What Edward didn't know, was Annie's memory had been coming back in bits and pieces for a while now. She was almost sure it wasn't her late husband that had attacked her. She even suspected that Roy could be the one who possibly even killed Thomas. She couldn't prove it, but, the puzzle was fitting together now, just a few pieces missing. She still didn't remember being raped that night, all she could remember was the sweaty hands and heavy body on her, and the smell of alcohol was there in her dreams, always. "God forbid if it was Roy," she would think, because it would just kill Edward or most likely destroy their marriage.

By this time Eddie Jr. was back outside happily looking over his new car, unaware of the trauma his mom was going through.

"Let's get you on the couch Annie, while I call Dr. Martin and see if he can come out and take a look at you. You don't look well at all!" As her husband was dialing the doctor's office, Annie had never felt so alone in her life; she was beginning to doubt her own sanity. She knew her husband did.

Dr. Martin had been Annie's family Doctor since they had moved to Kentucky, so he knew all the things she had been through. After examining her and talking for a while he told her she just needed to take it easy and prescribed a sedative. He told Edward it would help her sleep through the night, but told him to stay around close for a few days. In any case if she hadn't improved within a week he needed to see her in his office the following Wednesday.

Edward left Eddie with his mother while he drove the car back over to Roy's. On the way he racked his brain, trying to figure out why his wife would get such a thing in her head. He didn't know if he should say anything to his uncle about the things Annie had told him. After he thought about it, he decided to wait; there was no need to upset Uncle Roy needlessly. As it turned out, Roy wasn't at home and his truck wasn't in the drive, Edward figured he had an errand to run, so he parked the car back in the barn and left right away, not wanting to be away from his wife no longer than he had to.

*   *   *   *

A week had gone by and it seemed that Annie was doing better each day; therefore she didn't follow up with her doctor, even though Edward urged her to do so. He also hadn't heard from his uncle, he wondered if Uncle Roy sensed there was something going on about the car. He did act a little strange about taking the car over to show Annie that day. Edward remembered he had made the comment about getting it painted before taking it out.

That day Edward decided to drive over to see about him. Eddie was in school and Annie had gone grocery shopping. As he pulled in his uncle's drive he saw his old truck parked in the usual place. He didn't answer the door so Edward walked over to the barn, there he found Roy sanding on Eddies car. He looked surprised to see his nephew.

"Uncle Roy, I thought we were going to do this project together, you don't need to be tackling this by yourself."

"Well I thought the sooner we got started, the sooner

Eddie can be driving it. I know how it is when you're young." Roy said.

"Yea, I know, I'm sorry I hadn't been over for awhile, but Annie has been under the weather." He couldn't tell by his uncle's expression what he was thinking. Then Roy said. "She was upset by the car, wasn't she?"

"Why would you think that would bother her?" Edward asked, trying to get a reaction from him.

Roy slowly walked over to the rag box, tossing his cleaning rag in it. He sat down on an old wooden stool, but didn't say anything for a few minutes. Then he looked at Edward with sort of a questioning look in his eyes.

"Son, come over here and sit down, there's something I need to talk to you about."

Edward was shaking inside, not knowing what he was going to hear, but whatever it was, it wasn't going to be good. He just knew that.

Roy spoke in a low voice, just staring down at his faded old shoes. He started out telling Edward that he did know Annie back when her husband was alive, that he had helped Tom on the farm. He said the first time he saw Annie she was working in the garden, when she looked up; it was as if he was looking at a ghost. She was the spitting image of a girl he once knew, down to the color of her hair.

Edward knew the girl he was talking about, the one that had jilted him so many years ago.

He said he guessed she thought he was rude starring at her, but he couldn't help it. After that he wasn't around her except from a distance. He continued on, telling Edward that it was he that had taken Tom home that night. He had taken the old car out for a spin that day and had found Tom on the side of the road where his car had run out of gas. He said Tom looked pretty disoriented with blood all over his shirt, also he could smell alcohol on him. He drove Tom home and it was just as Annie had said that it was a brown car that had dropped him off. Roy told Edward that Tom was either still too drunk or the wound on his head made him so out of it that he didn't say anything, not even what had happened.

"Why didn't you tell the police that it was you that had dropped him off at his house that evening?"

"Because they never asked me anything about it, I never drove the car much, so they didn't know I had one; I guess. Besides that, I didn't want to get involved. All I did was take him home." Roy told Edward.

"But I swear I never harmed Tom in any way. He was always good to me. Later when I heard what had happened I was scared to go to the police, because apparently I was one of the last to see him alive."

Roy paused a second as if to think, before going on.

"I will tell you one thing, I'll never believe in a million years that Tom Flowers committed suicide, like some folks around here think." That was the first time Roy had looked up at Edward while telling him what he knew.

"Is all this the reason you seem so uncomfortable around Annie, Uncle Roy? Because she looks so much like the girl you were engaged to, or because she saw the brown car and could possibly recognize it if she saw it again?"

"Both, I guess, but in the beginning it was like seeing Beth after all those years. So I tried not to be around her after that, because it hurt so much remembering Beth. Besides I knew it was a matter of time she would do poor old Tom the way Beth did me."

"Then when you brought her over here to meet me I knew if I said anything to you it would make things worse. I just prayed she wouldn't recognize me, but she did, for she tried to tell me one day, and I just blew her off as if I didn't know what she was talking about. I guess in the back of my mind I thought that someday she would hurt you too." When Roy said that, Edward saw a look in his eyes that he had never seen before.

"You know you have been like a son to me, and then along came little Eddie. So I just went on keeping it to myself. I couldn't risk losing the two people that means the world to me. I knew when Eddie took the car over to show Annie, she would remember it. I knew then I would have to come clean." Roy was looking back down again, as if waiting for Edward to say something.

"Uncle Roy, I know you had nothing to do with what happened to Tom and Annie, but you should have talked to me and I would have gone to the police with you. They would have believed you just like I do."

"I don't know Edward, I just couldn't risk it."

"There is something else I need to say. I knew you were seeing Tom's wife at the time he died; I saw you together on the farm. I didn't want the police to know I was with Tom that day for fear they would suspect you. Maybe they would think you and me were in on it together."

"Uncle Roy, I was questioned like several others were, while Annie was in the hospital and I told them every thing about our relationship. Then after that, they pretty much ruled his death, self inflected. The police suspected he was so distraught after he realized what he had done to Annie; he just couldn't live with it. Annie has never remembered who beat her up, but she always thought it was Tom."

"The day you drove Tom home, did you see anyone strange around their farm, maybe a vehicle parked nearby?" Edward asked.

"I had no reason to be looking for anything out of the ordinary. I remember seeing Annie at the door; that's all."

Roy said he drove back home and parked the car back in the barn. The next day he heard what happened out at the Flower's farm, and that Tom was dead.

"What are you going to do Edward? Roy asked.

"After so many years that have gone by, I don't think it would do any good to go to the police now. Let me think about it and we will talk later."

Edward wanted to talk to his wife. He dreaded bringing up that awful time in her life, but he felt she needed to know.

It was as good a time as any when Edward got home to talk to Annie. She seemed to be in a better mood, which was good in one way, but on the other hand he hated to bring her down with all the things Roy had told him.

*   *   *   *

"Take your shoes off honey, I just mopped the floor." She said as Edward was about to come through the door. "You were over at Roy's quiet awhile. Is he ok?" she saw an expression on her husband's face that made her think he was worried about something.

"Oh, I guess he is ok," it's just some things he told me that I didn't know about."

"What things? Edward." Annie stopped what she was doing, waiting for her husband to tell her about Roy. Had Roy told her husband that it was he that drove Tom home that day? She asked Edward again, what was going on.

Annie listened as Edward told her word for word what was said between his uncle and him. After he finished, Annie didn't say anything for a while, when she did, she told her husband that he and Roy should go to the police and that she would go with them. She thought if it wasn't Tom that had beaten her almost to death, then there is someone running free to do it to someone else. Maybe, he already had.

Now that Annie understood why Roy had acted the way he did toward her, she felt sorry for him and guilty for thinking he had been responsible for everything; the girl really must have hurt him bad. She thought.

Edward and Annie did go to the police. They each told him what they knew. Sheriff Drew was initially the one that headed up the investigation at the murder scene as well as where Annie was attacked. Annie had told him when she came out of her coma about the brown car.

The police followed up on all the leads, but when there was no evidence of anyone being out there that day; the case went cold and later on they concluded it was Tom Flowers that committed the crimes.

Sheriff Drew didn't see any other reason to reopen the case, even after hearing about Roy taking Tom home. That alone proved nothing.

Annie wasn't convinced, she wanted to know who attacked her and then killed her husband. Also the other things that went on before that day, such as the animal hanging in the barn; as if it was a warning; Edward wanted to forget it all, he still believed it was Tom and he didn't want his wife to go through any more than she had already.

Annie wanted to find the person who was guilty, so she hired an investigator from Louisville to look into the case. It took less than a year for the private investigator to track down a man from Barren County. Jake Lee was arrested and convicted of the assault on Annie and the murder of Thomas Flowers. Lee admitted everything, he was near death and knew he had nothing to loose by telling the truth. He had met Thomas Flowers in a bar somewhere in Tennessee. They were both drunk by the time Tom left the bar that evening.

Lee said he followed Flowers with the intentions of robbing him. A few miles down the road, just across the Tennessee line, Lee found him parked on the side of the road, he looked as if he had passed out, so he picked up a jagged rock and hit Thomas across the head, just in case he did come around before he took what he could find. With all the blood spurting out, he thought he had killed him.

As he was stealing his wallet, Tom groaned and opened his eyes for a split second, so Lee got scared and drove away.

Then, when he realized Tom may not have died and could recognize him he took the address from the wallet and went to the Flowers home that night.

He said he had been drinking non-stop for weeks at that time, so all that he could remember was still like a bad dream and most of that day is a blank. What he did remember, was when he got to the Flowers house the back door was not locked, so he slipped in. The first bedroom he came to, he turned the knob of the door, it wasn't locked, but there was a wooden straight chair wedged under the knob to where it only opened an inch or two, so he knocked the door down. Instead of finding Tom inside, he heard a women screaming and a gun clicking, as if it was misfiring. He couldn't make out much for it was so dark. He then grabbed the rifle from the woman and hit her as hard as he could.

(Jake Lee never mentioned the fact that Annie was raped that night nor did he admit doing it. He wasn't questioned about it either because it was never reported to the police.)

Then he told the sheriff that the next thing he knew Tom Flowers jumped him. He also said that he was a lot bigger and stronger than Tom was back then, and it was easy to over power him. Lee said he still had the gun in his hands as he ran across a field with Flowers on his heels, they struggled and the gun went off, striking Tom in the head. After that, he put the weapon next to his body, making it look like a suicide. He thought he had gotten away with it. In a way he had, but he was a prisoner in his own body for over nineteen years.

The man that had shattered so many lives accidently shot himself while hunting, just a week or so after he killed Thomas, and he had been in a wheel chair ever since. He died within a month after he was arrested.

"Poetic Justice." Was what Annie called it.

But was it really? Maybe so for what Jake Lee had done; he did get what was coming to him, but there were unanswered questions as far as Edward was concerned. He wondered if Jake had told the whole story in his confession. He thought there was more to it than what Jake had claimed. Although he never knew about the rape he couldn't help but wonder if his uncle in some way had a hand in the attack on Annie.

Even though many years had passed and peoples memory of things change, yet, Edward kept thinking of what his uncle said about Tom being dead. No one knew

Tom was dead when they found Annie, so how did Roy know that?

Did Roy think because Annie looked so much like the girl that jilted him that she would do the same to his nephew?

The story Jake told made sense; up to a point, but Edward couldn't forget what his uncle told him. He would never know the answers to these questions, Jake was dead and he knew his uncle Roy would go to his grave with any answers he may or may not have.

As far as he knew his uncle and Jake Lee didn't even know each other, and if Jake told it all, why didn't he say that Roy was with him. Something just didn't ring true about it all. Jake did say he had been drinking for weeks, so maybe there was a blackout period he really didn't remember. Or maybe Roy was there afterwards to do away with Annie and saw it was already accomplished, or so he thought.

Edward knew his uncle thought a lot of Tom and in his somewhat twisted mind maybe he wanted to protect his nephew and his friend. Edward surmised, when he got there and saw Annie was not moving and the door was broken, maybe he thought Tom had killed her himself. It was possible Roy went looking for Tom and found his friend already dead as well. There was no misunderstanding, Roy told him about Tom being dead before he was even found. He had to have been there.

Edward never saw his uncle in the same light after

that. Then one day Roy got in his truck and drove away, never to be seen or heard from again.

And in time Edward gave up trying to figure it all out, saving all his energy and love for his son and Annie.

*   *   *   *

It had been three years since anyone had heard from Roy Barns, somewhat like the girl he was to marry had left years ago; never to be heard from again.

Edward had been out to his place several times over the years but there was never any sign of him being there. That made him look that much more guilty in the attack on Annie. Why else would he take off like that? Knowing how much Eddie Jr. thought of him.

Then one day a couple of men came to Edwards's house, they wanted to talk to Roy. When Edward told them he had not seen his uncle in three years, the men introduced themselves as, Detectives Abrams and Tidwell. Detective Abrams asked Edward if he cared to answer a few questions concerning his uncle.

He told them he would tell them what he could (expecting it was something to do with the Flowers case)

"Did Roy Barns ever tell you about a girl named Beth Trace?" Detective Abrams asked him.

"Well yes, as a matter of fact he had talked to me about her; they were going to be married but she left town. That's about all I know about her. Of course I wasn't even born at that time, so I never actually met her. What is this all about, Detective?"

"Do you know where your uncle is? I know you said you hadn't seen him, but I was wondering if maybe he had called and you have a number or an address?" It was Detective Tidwell, the older of the two asking the questions now.

"I am sorry, like I said I haven't seen him nor have I heard from him in over three years." Edward told them. Then he asked them again why they were looking for Roy.

"A few weeks ago bones were found by a road crew, and a tip we have is that the bones may belong to a Beth Trace, how the tipster knew that is beyond me, but the remains are at least fifty to sixty years old." He said they believed Roy was the last person to have seen her alive.

"We did some investigating and found out she was from here and knew Roy, we thought he may be able to help us find out who would have wanted her dead. A bullet hole was in her skull."

"I am sorry I can't help you fellows, but like I said, I really don't know where you could find him."

"One more question before we go, Mr. Barns; if you don't mind me asking. Why did Roy Barns leave town without telling anyone? He didn't even tell you, did he? Was he in any sort of trouble that you know of?" Detective Tidwell asked.

"Not that I know of." Edward told them. He knew he wasn't being completely honest because he suspected his uncle had something to do with attacking Annie, but speculation is all it was.

"Personally, I have a gut feeling your uncle is the one who identified the bones and made sure we got the tip." Detective Tidwell said as they were leaving. "Maybe to ease his conscience; just a feeling, mind you."

Edward wondered if he had ever really known his uncle.

He was thankful his son was away in collage so he wouldn't be hearing the tales going around about Roy, and that's exactly what will happen. Edward knew from the conversation with Tidwell and Abrams that they had talked to others around town.

When Annie came home, her husband told her about the men that were asking questions about Roy and his relationship with the girl he had told Annie about.

"Good Lord, do they think he did something to her?"

Annie felt the familiar chill run down her spine like it used to do when she caught Roy looking at her.

"That was the one who jilted him, wasn't it. But you said she left town. Why would they be interested in her? She has to be an old woman by now." Annie said.

"It seems bones were found which they think belong to Beth Trace." Edward told her in a whisper as if he was afraid someone would hear him say the unthinkable.

Just as Edward thought, everyone was talking and it was the top news bit every evening for weeks. They had Roy being anything from a serial killer to a hit man.

Finally something in the news topped that story and the gossip died down and the detectives never came back to talk to anyone in Kentucky.

Life was back to normal for the Barns family until one day they got a call from California. They were told that Roy Barns had passed away in a nursing home there. His living will named Edward as next of kin and all he had was left to Edward's son, Eddie Jr.

There was nothing else mentioned in the letter as to where he had been or why he had left in the first place.

Present day

When on a good day the old woman still takes a walk around the edge of the woods, especially during the fall when the wind blows through the colorful trees, tossing leaves around like confetti. A single leaf will sometimes get caught in the curls of her hair that is no longer the flaming red it used to be, but only a hint of what was, mixed with the gray that has replaced it.

Annie has outlived two husbands, Tom, her first love will cross her mind often, not the bad times they had, only the happy ones she chooses to remember; she found peace remembering Tom and their first years together; as clear as if yesterday she remembers going skinny dipping in the cool creek water after a hot day in the fields. The nightmares had vanished a long time ago. Yet deep in her heart guilt was a constant companion, reminding her of the part she played in her first husband's demise.

Edward, her last and forever love, will come to visit her while she is sleeping. That is when she is the happiest, walking hand and hand across a field of clover until they come to a place to rest, and with strong youthful hands he pulls her down beside him on a bed of green moss as she eagerly waits for their lips to touch, but first he will gently pull the ribbon from her beautiful long hair, allowing it to fall free around her bare shoulders as she looks into his eyes that are as blue as the sky.

The end